D0269097

THE WORLD OF ASTRID LINDGREN

PiPPi
LONGSTOCKING
AND THE SNIRKLE HUNT

OXFORD
UNIVERSITY PRESS

Great Clarendon Street, Oxford OX2 6DP
Oxford University Press is a department of the University of Oxford.
It furthers the University's objective of excellence in research, scholarship,
and education by publishing worldwide. Oxford is a registered trade mark of
Oxford University Press in the UK and in certain other countries

© Text: Astrid Lindgren 1948 The Astrid Lindgren Company
Illustrations by Ingrid Vang Nyman © The Astrid Lindgren Company

Pictures converted by Dave Shephard
Translated by Susan Beard

First published in 1948 by Rabén & Sjögren, Sweden as
a chapter of Pippi Långstrump i Söderhavet

For more information about Astrid Lindgren, see www.astridlindgren.com.
All foreign rights are handled by The Astrid Lindgren Company, Lidingö, Sweden.
For more information, please contact info@astridlindgren.se.

The moral rights of the author have been asserted

Database right Oxford University Press (maker)

First published in English as a chapter of Pippi Longstocking in the South Seas
First published in this edition 2020

All rights reserved. No part of this publication may be reproduced,
stored in a retrieval system, or transmitted, in any form or by any means,
without the prior permission in writing of Oxford University Press,
or as expressly permitted by law, or under terms agreed with the appropriate
reprographics rights organization. Enquiries concerning reproduction
outside the scope of the above should be sent to the Rights Department,
Oxford University Press, at the address above

You must not circulate this book in any other binding or cover
and you must impose this same condition on any acquirer

British Library Cataloguing in Publication Data

Data available

ISBN: 978-0-19-277243-5

1 3 5 7 9 10 8 6 4 2

Printed in China

Paper used in the production of this book is a natural,
recyclable product made from wood grown in sustainable forests.
The manufacturing process conforms to the environmental
regulations of the country of origin.

PiPPi
LONGSTOCKING
AND THE **SNIRKLE HUNT**

BY **ASTRID LINDGREN**
ILLUSTRATED BY
INGRID VANG NYMAN

OXFORD
UNIVERSITY PRESS

MEET THE CHARACTERS

Tommy

Annika

Pippi

Mr Nilsson

Pippi's horse

CHAPTER 1

Pippi Invents a New Word

One morning Tommy and Annika came skipping into Pippi's kitchen as usual and shouted good morning.

Pippi was sitting in the middle of
the kitchen table with Mr Nilsson,
the little monkey, in her arms and a
contented smile on her face.

'Morning,' said Tommy
and Annika again.

'Can you believe it?' said
Pippi, in a far-away voice. 'Can you
believe I'm the one who made it up?
Me and nobody else!'

'What have you made up?' asked
Tommy and Annika. It didn't surprise
them in the least that Pippi had made
something up because she always did,
but they wanted to know what it was.
'What exactly have you made up,
Pippi?'

'A new word,' said Pippi, and she looked at Tommy and Annika as if she had only just seen them. 'A brand spanking new word.'

'What is the word?' asked Tommy.

'A most excellent word,' said Pippi. 'One of the best I've ever heard.'

'Tell us, then,' said Annika.

'Snirkle,' Pippi said triumphantly.

'Snirkle,' said Tommy. 'What does it mean?'

'If only I knew,' said Pippi. 'The only thing I do know is that it doesn't mean dustbin lid.'

Tommy and Annika thought for a while. At last Annika said:

'But if you don't know what it means then it's not much use, is it?'

'No, that's what annoys me,' said Pippi.

'Who actually thought up from the beginning what words mean?' Tommy wondered.

'Most likely a load of old professors,' said Pippi. 'And people are very odd, I must say. Think of the words they make up! "Tongs" and "plug" and "string" and stuff. No one has a clue where they get them from. But they haven't bothered inventing "snirkle", which is a really good word. How lucky I came up with it! And I expect I'll find out what it means, too.'

She contemplated this for a few moments.

'Snirkle! Could it possibly mean the very, very top of a blue-painted flagpole, do you think?' she said uncertainly.

'There aren't any flagpoles painted blue,' said Annika.

'No, you're right. In that case I haven't the faintest idea. Could it possibly be the sound you make when you trample in the mud and it comes up between your toes? Let's give it a try: "Annika trampled around in the mud and it made the most wonderful snirkle."'

She shook her head.

'No, that doesn't work. "It made the most wonderful **SHBLURP**"– that's what it ought to be.'

She scratched her head.

'This is getting more and more mysterious. But I'll find out, whatever it is. Maybe you can buy it in a shop? Come on, let's go and ask.'

Tommy and Annika had nothing against doing that. Pippi went to find her travelling bag that was full of golden coins.

'Snirkle. Sounds expensive. I'd better take a whole golden coin.'

And so she did. Mr Nilsson hopped onto her shoulder as usual and then Pippi lifted her horse down from the veranda.

'No time to waste,' she said to Tommy and Annika. 'Let's ride. Otherwise there might not be many snirkles left when we get there. It wouldn't surprise me if the town mayor has already taken the last one.'

CHAPTER 2

Pippi at the Shops

When the horse came
galloping through the
streets of the little town
with Pippi and Tommy
and Annika on its back
its hooves clattered
so loudly that all the
children heard it, and
they came out to run
happily along beside it
because they all liked
Pippi very much.

'Pippi, where are you going?' they called.

'To buy a snirkle,' Pippi said, and pulled on the reins.

The children stopped running and looked baffled.

'Is it nice to eat?' a little boy asked.

'I should say so,' said Pippi, licking her lips. 'It's delicious. At least, it sounds like it is.'

She hopped off the horse outside a baker's shop and lifted down Tommy and Annika. In they went.

'I'd like a bag of snirkles, please,'
said Pippi. 'The crunchy kind.'

'Snirkles,' said the pretty assistant behind the counter, stopping to think. 'I don't think we've got any.'

'You must have,' said Pippi. 'You can find them in every well-stocked shop.'

'Ah, well, we've already sold out,' said the girl, who had never heard of snirkles but didn't want to admit that her shop wasn't as well-stocked as everyone else's.

'Does that mean you had them yesterday?' said Pippi excitedly. 'Please, please tell me what they looked like. I've never seen a snirkle in all my life. Did it have red stripes?'

The pretty assistant blushed charmingly and said:

'Oh dear, I don't know what they are! But we haven't got them here, anyway.'

Pippi walked back to the door, feeling very disappointed.

'Then I'll carry on searching,' she said. 'I'm not going home without a snirkle.'

The next shop was an ironmonger's. The assistant bowed to the children politely.

'I'd like to buy a snirkle,' Pippi said. 'But it must be the very best kind, the kind you kill lions with.'

The assistant looked crafty.

'Let me see,' he said, scratching behind his ear. 'Let me see.'

He found a garden rake
and held it out to Pippi.

'Will this do?' he asked.

Pippi gave him a withering look.

'That is what educated people call a
rake,' she said. 'But I happened to ask
you about a snirkle. Don't try fooling a
little innocent child!'

The assistant laughed and said:

'We haven't got one of those things
you asked for, unfortunately. Try the
haberdasher's on the corner.'

'The haberdasher's,' muttered Pippi. 'They won't have one there, I know that much.'

She looked gloomy for while, but then brightened up.

'Perhaps, when you think about it, a snirkle is an illness,' she said. 'Let's go and ask the doctor!'

CHAPTER 3

Pippi at the Doctor's

Annika knew where the doctor lived because she had been taken there for her vaccinations.

Pippi rang the bell. A nurse came and opened the door.

'Is the doctor in?' asked Pippi. 'It's a very urgent case. A tremendously serious disease.'

'Do come in. This way,' said the nurse.

The doctor was sitting at his desk when the children came in. Pippi walked straight up to him, closed her eyes and stuck out her tongue.

'And what is the matter with you?'
asked the doctor.

Pippi opened wide her clear blue
eyes and pulled in her tongue.

'I'm afraid I've got an attack of the snirkles,' she said. 'I'm itching all over and my eyelids slam shut when I go to sleep. Sometimes I hiccup. And last Sunday I felt a bit poorly after I'd eaten a bowl of shoe polish and milk. Nothing wrong with my appetite but my food always goes the wrong way so it doesn't do me much good. I must have got an attack of the snirkles. Tell me one thing: is it catching?'

The doctor looked at Pippi's healthy little face and said:

'I think you are healthier than most. I'm certain you're not suffering from the snirkles.'

Pippi grabbed his arm, eagerly.

'So there is an illness called that?'

'No,' said the doctor. 'There isn't.

But even if it did exist, I don't think it would give you any trouble.'

Pippi looked glum. She curtseyed deeply to the doctor by way of saying goodbye, and Annika did the same.

Tommy bowed. Then they walked back to the horse that was waiting in the doctor's garden.

CHAPTER 4

Pippi Climbs Up

Not far from the doctor's house was a block of flats three floors high. A window on the top floor was open. Pippi pointed up at the open window and said:

'It wouldn't surprise me if there was a snirkle inside there. I'll pop up and have a look.'

And quick as a wink she shinned up the drainpipe. When she came level with the window she threw herself headlong into thin air and caught hold of the windowsill.

She pulled herself up and thrust
in her head.

Two ladies were sitting in the room
inside, chatting.

Guess how astonished they were
to see a red head suddenly appear
above the windowsill, and
hear a voice saying:

'Just wondering, is
there a snirkle in here?'

The two ladies
shrieked in horror.

'Heavens above,
child, what are
you saying? Has
someone escaped?'

'That's precisely what I would like to know,' said Pippi politely.

'Oh, perhaps he's under the bed?'
cried one of the ladies.
'Does he bite?'

'Highly likely,' said Pippi. 'It sounds like he's got a good set of teeth.'

The two ladies clung to each other. Pippi scrutinized the room but finally said regretfully:

'No, not even a snirkle's whisker. Sorry for interrupting! I thought I'd enquire, seeing as I happened to be passing.'

She slid back down the drainpipe.

CHAPTER 5

Pippi Finds a Snirkle

'Pity,' Pippi said to Tommy and Annika.
'There's no snirkle in this town. Let's
ride home again.'

And that's what they did. As they jumped down from the horse outside the veranda Tommy almost trampled on a little beetle that was scuttling along the gravel path.

'Oh, mind the beetle!' shouted Pippi.

All three crouched down to look at him. He was so small. His wings were green and gleamed like metal.

'What a beautiful little thing,' said Annika. 'I wonder what kind it is?'

'It's not a May beetle,' said Tommy. 'Or a dung beetle either. And not a stag beetle. I really wish I knew what kind it was.'

A delighted smile spread across Pippi's face.

'I know,' she said. 'It's a snirkle.'

'Are you sure?' asked Tommy doubtfully.

'Do you think I can't recognize a snirkle when I see one?' said Pippi.

'Have you ever seen anything more snirkle-like in your life?'

Carefully she moved the beetle to a safer place where he wouldn't get trampled on.

'My sweet little snirkle,' she said, tenderly. 'I knew I'd find one in the end. But how odd. We've been running around town looking for a snirkle and there was one here all the time, right outside Villa Villekulla.'

HOW WELL DO YOU KNOW PIPPI LONGSTOCKING?

Her full name is Pippilotta Victoriaria Tea-cosy Appleminta Ephraim's-daughter Longstocking.

She lives with her monkey, Mr Nilsson, who was a present from her father.

She can walk a tightrope and even do 43 somersaults in a row.

Pippi can climb up a ladder backwards and even eat pears hanging upside down from a tree.

When Pippi sleeps, she always puts her feet on the pillow and her head under the covers.

She's so strong she can lift a horse over her head.

SPOT THE DIFFERENCE

Can you spot five diferences
between these pictures?

The answers are on the last page.

HAVE ANOTHER ADVENTURE WITH PIPPI LONGSTOCKING!

Who is Pippi Longstocking? She's so strong she can lift a horse. So clever she can outsmart robbers. So fun she can plan the best birthday party ever! Pippi Longstocking can do anything! She lives on her own with a monkey and a horse, and there's nobody to tell her to be sensible. Life is one big adventure with Pippi—once you meet her you'll want to play with her every day!

TWO-
COLOUR RED
AND BLACK
ILLUSTRATION

THE WORLD OF ASTRID LINDGREN

MEET

Pippi
LONGSTOCKING

ILLUSTRATED BY
INGRID VANG NYMAN

978-0-19-277242-8

THE WORLD OF ASTRID LINDGREN

Want to read more about Pippi? Discover the three classic Pippi books – packed with extraordinary adventures and exploits, all in Pippi's own unforgettable style!

Now with stunning new
black and white illustrations
from Mini Grey.

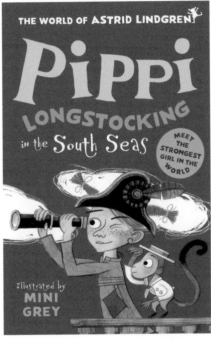

THE WORLD OF
ASTRID LINDGREN

Meet Astrid Lindgren's other wonderful characters, and enter their world of freedom, fun, and outdoor adventures.

EMIL

The angelic-faced boy with a talent for trouble!

KARLSSON

When Karlsson flies into Smidge's life, things will never be dull again . . .

LOTTA

Small, stubborn, and full of ideas. . .

THE CHILDREN OF NOISY VILLAGE

Six children and a world of free-range fun!

ABOUT THE AUTHOR

Astrid Lindgren was born in 1907, and grew up at a farm called Näs in the south of Sweden. Her first book was published in 1944, followed a year later by *Pippi Longstocking*. She wrote 34 chapter books and 41 picture books, that all together have sold 165 million copies worldwide. Her books have been translated into 107 different languages and according to UNESCO's annual list, she is the 18th most translated author in the world.

ABOUT THE ILLUSTRATOR

Ingrid Vang Nyman was born in 1916 in Vejen in southern Jylland, in Denmark. She took her work as an illustrator very seriously, worked very fast and had a high level of ambition. She demanded that illustrations for children should be of the same high artistic quality as for adults.

Ingrid Vang Nyman was *Pippi Longstocking*'s original illustrator and her classic artwork is recognized worldwide.

Answers to spot the difference: The horse's stomach band is missing; Pippi's patch on her top has moved; The rider is smiling; Pippi has two plaits; The horse is spotty.